Ghost in the Mirror

Look for more books in the Goosebumps Series 2000
by R.L. Stine:

Ghost in the Mirror

AN
APPLE
PAPERBACK

SCHOLASTIC INC.
New York Toronto London Auckland
Sydney New Delhi Hong Kong

A PARACHUTE PRESS BOOK

ISBN-13: 978-0-439-13535-1

This edition is for sale in Indian subcontinent only.

First Scholastic printing, January 2000
Reprinted by Scholastic India Pvt. Ltd., September 2007
March 2008; January; August 2010; May 2011; January 2012
July; September; December 2013; September; December 2014; July 2015

Printed at Magic International, Greater Noida

"YOU LOSE!"

The deafening cry made me jump into the air. My heart pounded against my chest.

I spun around to find my sister, Claudia, laughing. Her dark eyes flashed behind her red-framed glasses. Her mouth was open wide in a toothy grin, and I could see her red-and-blue braces gleaming in the hall light.

"Claudia, give me a break." I groaned. "Stop scaring me all the time. It isn't that funny."

"I know," she replied, tugging at a tangle in her thick black hair. "It's not funny. It's sad. You're no challenge, Jason. You're too easy to scare."

My name is Jason Sloves, and I'm your basic wimp.

Well . . . that's not exactly true.

1

You'd scream a lot too if you had an older sister who was always sneaking up behind you, leaping out of closets, putting ice-cold hands on the back of your neck, and doing everything she could to scare you.

Actually, I'm *not* a wimp. I'm a normal guy with a crazy sister.

Do you know the word *demented*? If you look it up in the dictionary, you'll see a picture of Claudia there.

Two years ago, when I was ten and Claudia was twelve, she found a dead rat in the basement. She tied a fishing line around its neck, hid it under my bed, and told me I had a rat living beneath my bed. When I peeked under the bed, she pulled the line and made the rat come scrambling toward me.

I screamed a lot.

Maybe I screamed more than most kids would.

But that's *demented* — right?

My best friend, Fred, agrees. He can't understand why Claudia is always flashing those red-and-blue braces at everyone, always snapping the rubber bands, and clicking her teeth at people.

She's crazy. How else can you explain it?

A few months ago, she sneaked into my room and hid strands of spaghetti under my covers. Of *course* I screamed when I climbed into bed and felt them wriggling on my back.

I thought they were snakes — wouldn't *you*?

Demented.

Not to mention disturbed.

Now she stood in the hallway, hands on her waist, tossing her black mop of hair from side to side as she grinned at me. "You lose, Jason. I knew you couldn't do it."

"Couldn't do *what*?" I asked. Claudia is always betting me this, betting me that. So many bets, who could keep track?

"Yesterday I bet that you couldn't pass by a mirror without looking into it," Claudia said. She pointed to the hall mirror behind me. "You lose."

"I was just checking my hair," I replied. I have thick black hair like Claudia's, and it's always messed up. It's like on springs or something. Always bouncing.

"You were admiring yourself as always," Claudia sneered. "You think you're so cool-looking."

"No, I don't," I protested.

I really don't. I hate my bouncy, messed-up hair. And I hate my round head and my big, baby-face cheeks that Mom can't help but pinch.

Claudia picked up Buzzy, our little brown dog, and started to pet him. He's a tiny mutt, part terrier, part who-knows-what. He's very furry. In fact, his eyes are covered with fur. I have no idea how Buzzy sees!

"You can't pass a mirror without checking yourself out," Claudia insisted.

3

"Give me a break," I repeated.

I didn't want to argue with her. What's the point? She's demented!

I turned and started up the stairs to my room.

I thought maybe I'd call my friend Fred and see if he wanted to come over and play some video games. But Claudia wasn't finished with me. She followed me into my room, carrying Buzzy.

"Beat it," I said. I tried to push her to the door, but she's bigger than me.

"You have a baby room," she said. She flashed her red-and-blue grin again.

"Beat it, Claudia."

I do have a baby room. But there's nothing I can do about it.

I covered the walls with some really outstanding WWF posters. But they don't hide my light blue baby dresser and my little blue bed.

"Why don't you just sleep in your old crib?" Claudia said. Then she tossed back her head and laughed as if she'd made a really funny joke.

"Stop it, Claudia!"

We both turned to find Mom in the doorway.

She frowned at Claudia. "Why are you making fun of Jason?"

Claudia shrugged. "Because he's a big baby?"

"I am *not!*" I cried. I didn't mean to whine. It just came out that way.

"You *know* why he still has some of his baby furniture," Mom told Claudia. "We can't afford new furniture — can we? You know your dad has been out of work for nearly a year."

Claudia lowered her head and pretended to be sorry. "Yes, I know." She set Buzzy down.

The little mutt scampered out of the room. He didn't like arguments or loud voices.

"So why give Jason a hard time about his furniture?" Mom asked her.

Claudia grinned. "Why not?"

Mom sighed. "Claudia, I wish you'd try to be nicer to your brother."

"Okay, Mom," Claudia replied. "No problem. I'll try."

Mom made her way downstairs.

Claudia pointed to the window. "Look out! There's a *hornet* in the room!"

"Huh?" I cried. "Where? Where?"

About two weeks later, Fred and I were tossing a football back and forth in the front yard. Well ... actually, I was tossing it and Fred was chasing it.

Fred isn't very good at sports.

He's tall and lanky. Everyone always asks him if he's on the basketball team.

But Fred couldn't run *and* dribble the ball if his life depended on it. Even when he's *walking*, he falls over his own Nikes!

Fred has tiny bright blue eyes, blond hair shaved like peach fuzz on his head, and a sort of crooked, goofy smile. He's a good guy. He's smart and a lot of fun. He's just not an athlete.

It was after school on a cool fall Friday afternoon, and we were slipping and sliding on the fallen leaves.

I sent a long pass sailing toward the street. Fred took off after it, his skinny arms stretched out in front of him, hands reaching, reaching . . .

Fred went down and slid across the grass on his belly to catch it. But, of course, the ball bounced off his fingertips into the street.

I wanted to shout, "How could you miss that one, you clumsy klutz?" But he's my best friend. So instead, I called out, "Nice try!"

Then I turned to the house and saw Mom and Dad waving to me from the front door.

"Jason, come check this out!" Dad called. "Hurry. We have a surprise for you."

And that's when all the trouble began.

2

red had to go home. So I said good-bye to him and trotted up the front lawn to the house.

Mom and Dad had smiles on their faces and seemed pretty excited. "What's going on?" I asked.

"Follow us," Mom said.

We raced up the stairs to my room. Mom and Dad stopped out in the hallway and pushed me inside.

"Wow!" I exclaimed.

"We made a few improvements," Dad said, resting a hand on my shoulder.

"Wow," I repeated.

My baby dresser was gone. In its place stood a big wooden dresser, kind of banged-up and chipped. An antique, I guessed.

Next to the dresser was a tall mirror. It stretched nearly from the floor to the ceiling.

"I know the dresser is a wreck," Dad said. "But we can fix it up. You know. Sand it down and put a new finish on it. It'll look like new."

"We found it at a garage sale," Mom said. "The nice thing is, it's big enough to hold all of your clothes. No more piling things on the closet floor."

"The bottom drawers are jammed shut," Dad said. "But I'll work on them as soon as I get a chance."

"It's great!" I said.

But I was more interested in the tall antique mirror.

I stood in front of it and gazed at my reflection.

"It's so . . . clear," I murmured.

The glass was clean and smooth and perfect.

The reflection was incredibly bright, almost brighter and clearer than the room.

A chill ran down my back.

There's something *wrong* here, I suddenly thought.

Something *weird*.

Why can't I take my eyes away from the mirror?

Why do I feel as if it is holding me here? Forcing me to look?

Why do I feel that the mirror is pulling me . . . pulling me to it?

That night, Fred came over and I showed off my new mirror and dresser.

Fred wasn't real impressed. "At least you got rid of the baby dresser," he said. "But this thing is kind of a wreck, isn't it?"

"Yeah. Some of the drawers are stuck. But that's okay. Dad and I are going to sand the dresser down and paint it," I told him.

I couldn't help glancing in the new mirror. I smiled at myself and saw something green stuck to my front tooth. I rubbed it off.

"Cool mirror, huh?" I said. I liked the way it reflected my WWF posters. It made my room look twice as big with posters all around.

"Did you watch the wrestling show on cable last night?" Fred asked.

"Of course," I replied. "Wasn't that awesome when they all started fighting in the audience?"

"And then those two geeks from the audience tried to get into the fight!" Fred laughed his high giggle. When he laughed, his eyes always closed, and his skinny shoulders bounced up and down.

We sat down in front of the old TV that my video game player is hooked up to. I turned my back to the new mirror so that I wouldn't be distracted by it.

We started to play an NBA basketball game. The sad thing was, Fred was as bad at *video* basketball as he was at real basketball.

I enjoyed playing with him, but it was never much of a contest. I always won. Usually by at least thirty points.

The game is really fast, just like a real basketball game. You've got to move your players down the floor, shoot fast, go up for rebounds, play a lot of defense.

We were punching our controllers hard, using both hands.

"Shoot! Shoot!" I cried to Fred.

His thumb attacked the "shoot" button on his controller. On the screen, his player heaved the ball over the basket, out of the court.

"Air ball," Fred groaned. "Just like in real life."

"Go for the steal," I told him. "Move that way. *That* way!"

I was always trying to help him, trying to make him better at it so that our games would be closer.

I hit the controller frantically. Stole the ball from Fred's player. Dribbled down the floor and sank an easy layup. The crowd on the screen cheered. The score changed.

"Fred — it's your ball," I said. "Hey —"

Fred was staring over my shoulder.

"What's wrong?" I asked.

"Sorry." He returned his eyes to the TV screen and began pushing buttons.

But I saw that he kept glancing toward the mirror.

Finally, I pushed PAUSE. The game was nearly over anyway. The score was sixty to twenty-four. Guess whose favor.

I set my controller on the carpet in front of me. "Fred, what's wrong?"

"The mirror," he said softly.

I turned. "What about it?"

"I — I saw something moving in there."

I frowned at him. "You mean like one of us?"

Fred shook his head. "No. Something else. It was weird."

I stared into the mirror. My reflection stared back. On the floor beside me, I could see Fred, his tiny blue eyes frightened.

"You're crazy," I said. "It's just us. What could be moving in the mirror?"

Fred shrugged. "Beats me."

The phone rang. It was Fred's mom. He had to go home.

I followed him downstairs and closed the door after him. It had started to rain, but he didn't have far to go. Fred lives on the next block.

I went into the kitchen and collected a handful of Oreos and a Coke. Then I made my way back to my room.

I planned to play another basketball game, this time against the machine. The machine was better than Fred. In fact, it was *too* good. I could seldom beat it.

I set down the cookies and the can of soda. Then I spotted something on the floor in front of the mirror.

I bent down and picked it up. A piece of paper. Folded up.

It was yellowed and stained and felt crinkly, as if it were really old.

I unfolded it carefully. And found a note inside.

A note written in black ink in old-fashioned-looking, fancy handwriting.

Holding it close to my face, I read it out loud:

"BEWARE. BRING THIS INTO YOUR HOUSE — AND YOU BRING DEATH!"

I stared hard at the note. I read it again. Again.

Then I raised my eyes to the mirror. I saw myself standing there, my face tight with concern.

Did this note fall from behind the mirror?

What does it mean?

How did it get on the floor?

"Oh." I suddenly knew how the note got on the floor.

I watched my expression change in the mirror. Watched my face grow red with anger.

"Claudia!" I called. "I know you're out there, Claudia! I know you did this!"

I heard footsteps from Claudia's room down the hall. She came into the room all wide-eyed and innocent. "Did you call me, Jason?"

13

I held the note up and shook it. "Ha ha. Very funny," I said.

She scrunched up her face. "What's funny?"

"The note you wrote. Trying to scare me."

She stared at the yellowed paper in my hand. "You're crazy," she said. "That isn't mine."

I rolled my eyes. "I suppose it fell out from inside the mirror."

"Well, what is it?" she asked. She snatched it from my hand and read it quickly.

Her mouth dropped open. Behind her red glasses, her eyes went wide.

"Jason —" she whispered. "The mirror — it's HAUNTED!"

"Stop it!" I cried. "Stop it, Claudia. Don't try to scare me again." I studied her face. "You're kidding — right?"

"N-no," she whispered. Then she turned and pointed to the mirror. "There he is! There's the ghost!"

I let out a cry.

My hand shot out and knocked over the Coke can. The soda poured onto my carpet.

I dropped to the floor and grabbed the can.

I heard Claudia laughing as she made her way to the hall. "You're too easy, Jason. You're just too easy to scare!"

"And you're not funny!" I called angrily. "I thought you were going to be nicer to me. I thought you were going to give me a break!"

She didn't answer. I heard her bedroom door close.

I mopped up the spilled Coke. As I worked, I kept glancing into the mirror.

I didn't see anything strange in there. Just my own reflection, bright and clear, as clear and real as the real me.

15

I read the note again. Did Claudia write it?

I didn't think so. It *was* the kind of dumb trick she'd pull. But it wasn't her handwriting.

Besides, Claudia always admitted to her jokes. She was proud of them. She never acted innocent.

So where did the frightening note come from?

I folded it up carefully and carried it downstairs. I found Dad on his knees in the living room, trying to repair a broken electrical outlet.

"Dad — check this out," I said. I waited for him to set down his tools. Then I handed him the note.

He read the note quickly, then climbed to his feet. He cupped his hands around his mouth and started to shout. "Claudia? Claudia — get downstairs! Right now!"

"Of course, Claudia denied writing it," I told Fred. "And I think she was telling the truth."

I kicked the ball along the grass, a slow roller. But Fred's feet got tangled and he fell over the ball instead of kicking it back.

It was the next day, a cold gray afternoon, the air heavy and damp. We were kicking a soccer ball back and forth across the front yard.

I'm on a soccer team at school. Not the varsity team. Just intramural stuff. But I like soccer. It's actually my best sport.

I keep telling Fred he should play in our league. There are a lot of really bad, klutzy players.

That didn't exactly encourage him.

16

"Maybe the note was pinned to the back of the mirror," Fred said. He kicked the soccer ball hard off the side of his shoe. It flew high, bounced once, and landed in the hedge in front of the house.

"But why would anyone write a message like that?" I asked, chasing after the ball.

"Probably just a joke," Fred replied.

I leaned into the hedge and lifted the soccer ball out carefully. I turned to kick it to Fred — but stopped when I heard a noise.

Barking. Loud dog barking from inside the house.

Buzzy?

"What's his problem?" I asked. "Buzzy never barks."

I tossed the ball toward Fred. He actually caught it for once.

Somewhere inside the house, Buzzy was barking frantically.

"No one else is home," I said. "I'd better see what's freaking Buzzy out."

I ran around the side of the house and in through the back door. "Buzzy? Hey — Buzzy?" I called.

Buzzy only barks when he's frightened or really excited. And then he lets out these high, shrill barks that sound more like a mouse than a dog.

"Buzzy? Where are you?"

I followed the shrill dog squeals upstairs. I found Buzzy in my room.

He was sniffing the front of my new mirror. He sniffed the glass. Then he shot back a few steps and snapped his furry head up, barking furiously.

"Buzzy — stop!" I called, hurrying across the room.

But the dog stepped forward again. Sniffed the mirror. Barked shrilly. Stared into the glass, very upset.

"What is it? What do you see in there?"

I bent down and grabbed the little guy around the middle. "Come on. Let's go outside."

But he tugged me toward the mirror, barking, barking his little head off.

I picked him up and tried to calm the poor dog.

What did he see in there? What upset him so much?

Was he barking at his own reflection?

Fred had seen something moving in the mirror.

Did Buzzy see it too?

I told Mom and Dad about Buzzy at dinner, but they just laughed. They think everything Buzzy does is funny.

They were in a really good mood. Dad was hired for a job he'd been trying to get for months. "It's only a twenty-minute drive," he announced, "which means we don't have to move."

That made Claudia very happy.

Ever since Dad has been out of work, Claudia has worried that we'd have to move and go to a different school. She's so popular at school and has so many good friends, she was desperate not to move away.

Lucky Claudia.

I was happy for Dad. But I wasn't finished talking about Buzzy and the mirror. "Doesn't anyone think it's strange that Buzzy was barking like that?" I asked.

"Dogs often bark at mirrors," Mom replied, passing the fried chicken bucket. "They don't understand mirrors."

"Dogs are stupid," Claudia chimed in. "I read in a magazine that the really smart ones have IQs of ten."

I scooped some more mashed potatoes onto my plate. "He was acting really weird," I insisted. "It wasn't normal barking or anything. I think he saw something in the mirror and —"

"Are you going to bring up that note again?" Mom interrupted. "I told you, Jason — someone was playing a very mean joke with that note."

"Don't look at me!" Claudia cried. She swallowed a chunk of chicken, then gazed across the table at me. "I wrote a story about your mirror today."

I narrowed my eyes at her. "Excuse me?"

"In English class. We had to write a fictional story about a real object. So I made up a story about the mirror. It was pretty good. I called it 'The Haunted Mirror.'"

My mouth dropped open. "Haunted? Why haunted?"

"Jason, take it easy," Mom said. "Claudia is just teasing you."

"No, I'm not," Claudia insisted. "I really wrote it. It's about a young girl who died a hundred years ago. And her ghost lived inside the mirror. But she got bored in there. So one night, she sneaked out of the mirror . . . and silently crept across the bedroom . . . and floated over the boy who now owned the mirror . . ."

Claudia lowered her voice to a whisper. "And she lowered her ghostly spirit into the boy . . . and took over his body . . ." Claudia grinned at me.

"That sounds good," Dad said.

"That's very imaginative, Claudia," Mom added. "What happens next?"

"I don't know," Claudia told her. "That's as far as I got. The bell rang." She picked up a chicken leg and started chewing it.

"That's a dumb story," I said. "It's not even a *little* scary."

Claudia stared hard at me. "Maybe it's a *true* story," she said. "Maybe that's who wrote the mysterious note. The ghost of the girl who's trapped in the mirror."

"Claudia, stop trying to scare Jason," Mom scolded.

"Don't worry. She's not scaring me," I said.

"BOO!" Claudia yelled. "Ha ha. Made you jump."

"I did not!" I protested.

"You can both stop anytime," Mom said, gazing from Claudia to me. "This is supposed to be a celebration tonight, remember? Your father's new job?"

21

"How about a toast?" Dad suggested, raising his water glass. "A toast to *me*!"

Laughing, we all raised our water glasses.

We still had them raised when we heard the angry animal growls.

I nearly dropped my glass. "Is that Buzzy?"

Another furious growl floated into the room.

Mom jumped to her feet. "That can't be. Buzzy doesn't growl like that."

Dad lowered his glass to the table. "Did another dog get into the house?"

I pushed my chair back and stood up as we heard a furious snarl. "It's coming from upstairs. I'll go check it out."

That animal snarl was really scary. But I didn't want Claudia to know I was afraid.

So I ran up the stairs. "Buzzy? Buzzy — is that you?"

I grabbed the door frame and whirled myself into the bedroom.

Buzzy stood hunched with his back to the mirror.

"*Grrrrrrrr.*"

As I took a step into my room, my little dog pulled back his lips, baring his teeth. And growled from deep in his throat.

"Buzzy?"

I stared down at him. Why did he look so different?

Was it the way he hunched so low, with his legs bent as if ready to attack?

Was it the way his normally soft fur bristled up and down his back?

"Buzzy?"

I dropped to my knees and motioned for the dog to come to me. "It's okay, boy. It's okay."

He growled again.

As he lowered his head, his eyes glowed from beneath the furry bangs. Cold, dark eyes.

Not Buzzy's eyes.

"Buzzy, it's okay, boy," I called. "Buzzy — what's wrong?"

I didn't have time to move.

I didn't have a chance to stand up.

The dog sprang across the floor.

Leaped high.

And sank his teeth into my throat.

"Oooo!"

I uttered a choked scream and fell onto my back. I struggled to grab the dog, to pull him off me.

But grunting and growling, Buzzy clamped his teeth on my throat and clawed at my face with his front paws.

"Off, boy! Off!"

I felt warm blood run down my neck. Pain shot down my throat and chest.

The dog snapped at my ear. Raked a sharp paw down the side of my face.

"Help me! Somebody!" I screamed.

I grabbed Buzzy around the middle and pulled.

He snapped his jaw, snapped so viciously, so furiously.

My face throbbed with pain.

"HELP ME!"

I heard heavy footsteps on the stairs.

"Jason?" I saw the shock on Dad's face as he stopped to stare from the doorway.

And then he dove into the room and grabbed the snarling, clawing, snapping dog. Dad struggled for a moment. Buzzy suddenly had startling strength!

Finally, Dad pulled the dog off me. He lifted him high and held him out in front of him.

Buzzy kicked and squirmed, snapping his jaw like an alligator.

"What happened? What happened?" Dad cried, struggling to hold on to the raging animal.

I groaned in reply. I pulled myself shakily to my feet. "He — he just *attacked* me!"

The dog bent itself in half, snapping at Dad's hands. "He scratched you pretty bad, Jason," Dad said, shouting over the dog's loud snarls. He gave me a concerned look. "Go get yourself cleaned up. I'll take the dog away."

I staggered to the bathroom, ducked my head into the sink, and let the cold water run over my throbbing cheek. Over the trickle of the water, I could hear Buzzy barking and growling as Dad carried him downstairs.

I dried off my face. The scratches weren't too deep. The cut on my throat had already stopped bleeding.

I suddenly felt weak. And shaky. My legs were

trembling. I leaned on the sink to keep from col-
lapsing.

"What happened to Buzzy?" I asked my reflection in the medicine cabinet mirror.

The dog had always been so quiet, so gentle. He
hardly ever barked. He liked everyone in the fam-
ily. He would never even chase a *bird*!

I checked myself out one more time. Brushed
my hair into place. Then, feeling a little more normal, I made my way back to the dining room.

Mom and Claudia were still at the table.
"Where's Dad?" I asked.

"He took Buzzy outside," Mom said, biting her
bottom lip. "He's going to lock Buzzy in the
garage. Until he calms down."

"You don't think he caught rabies, do you?" I
asked my mom. I knew dogs with rabies acted
crazy — the way Buzzy was acting.

"I don't think so, honey," my mom answered.
"Dogs with rabies tend to foam at the mouth. I
didn't see Buzzy doing that."

"I — I don't understand it," I whispered. "What
could have happened?"

Claudia leaned across the table. Behind her
glasses, her eyes flashed with excitement. "Something up there sure scared him," she said softly.
"Something scared him really bad."

8

"Buzzy didn't look the same," I told Fred. "His fur was standing on end. Even his eyes were different."

"Weird," Fred muttered.

We were in my room later that night. We sat cross-legged on the carpet, game controllers in our laps, trying out a new hockey game. We had just started the game, and I was already beating Fred four goals to one.

"He scratched you pretty good," Fred said, pointing to my cheek. "Does it hurt?"

"A little," I replied.

I guided my player over the ice. Pulled back his stick. Took a shot.

Missed.

"How did such a little dog jump up to your

face?" Fred asked. He went for the puck. His player skated right past it.

"I got down on my knees," I told him.

"Smart move," Fred replied, rolling his blue eyes.

"Well, I didn't know he was going to *attack* me!" I cried.

I shot again. Fred's goalie threw himself onto his stomach and saved the goal.

"Hey — way to go!" I congratulated him.

"Just lucky," he said.

"I hope Buzzy will be okay," I said. Even through the closed window, I could hear his angry barking from inside the garage.

"He'll calm down," Fred said, missing a shot by a mile. "He probably just saw a mouse or something."

"A mouse?"

Why would that turn a sweet little dog into a vicious, snarling attacker?

Sometimes I worried about Fred. . . .

We stopped talking and leaned toward the TV screen, watching our players slide over the video ice. We played until our thumbs hurt from pushing the controllers so hard.

"Let's take a break," I said.

Fred groaned. "That's not fair. Just when I was starting to catch up!"

The score was twelve to one.

I set my controller on the floor. "Maybe we

should try a different kind of game," I suggested. "Maybe a racing game. There's a really cool off-road racing game I saw in a magazine."

Fred sighed. "I'd probably just crack up my car on the first turn."

He climbed to his feet and stretched his long, skinny arms. "Maybe I'd be better at some kind of battle game. I'm just not into sports that much."

He wandered over to the wall mirror and stared at himself. "This mirror is so . . . clear. It's like everything is clearer than in real life."

He made a face at himself. He stuck out his tongue.

Suddenly, his expression changed. His mouth dropped open. He motioned to me. "Hey, Jason?"

"What?" I stood up.

"Come here. Hurry."

I made my way to the mirror. And followed Fred's stare.

We both gazed into the mirror. We both saw it.

And we both screamed.

uzzy?

We both saw Buzzy's reflection in the mirror.

But how could that be?

In the glass, he stood between us, his head lowered, his eyes covered by his brown furry bangs. His ears were down, flat against his head, the way they got whenever he was frightened. His four spindly legs trembled.

"Buzzy?"

I turned away from the mirror and looked down at the floor.

No. He wasn't there.

I turned back to the mirror — and saw his reflection.

I swallowed hard. "It — it's impossible."

Fred nodded. His mouth opened but no sound came out.

I spun around and searched the whole bedroom. No. No sign of Buzzy.

My heart pounding, I turned back to the mirror.

Buzzy was still there in the glass, head lowered, ears down, tail between his legs.

"No," I whispered. "It can't be."

I took a deep breath and shouted out to the hall. "Claudia? Claudia — are you in your room?"

I heard her bedroom door open. Music poured into the hall. "What do you want?" she called, shouting over the sound.

"Come here! Hurry!"

A few seconds later, Claudia walked into the room. Her hair was piled high in pink plastic curlers. She crossed her arms in front of her. "I've got a lot of homework, Jason. What do you want?"

"Look —" I said, pointing. "In the mirror. Look."

Claudia frowned and stepped up beside Fred and me. "What's the big deal?"

Then she turned and gazed into the mirror.

And her mouth dropped open.

"You're in trouble, Jason," she murmured.

31

10

She swung around and shoved me. "Are you trying to be funny?"

"N-no," I said. "Look —"

I turned back to the mirror and stared down at the reflection of the floor.

Buzzy?

No. No sign of him now. No dog in the mirror.

Claudia shoved me again. "What's the joke? Why did you call me in here?"

Fred came to my rescue. "It was Buzzy. We saw him. In the mirror."

Claudia rolled her eyes. "Yeah. Sure."

"No — really!" I insisted.

"Buzzy is in the garage," Claudia said. "Hear him?"

Yes. I could hear him barking out there.

"But I saw his reflection in the mirror," I said. "Fred saw him too. We both did."

Claudia shook her head. She started toward the door. "You're both pitiful. Did you really think you could fool me with something that *lame*?"

She turned at the door and sneered at me. "You're such a wimp, Jason. Did my ghost story really scare you that much? You're twelve years old. You don't really think your room is *haunted* — do you?"

I didn't answer. I let her stomp back to her room.

When I heard her door slam, I turned back to Fred. "We really saw it, didn't we?"

Fred shrugged. "I — I guess. Maybe . . ."

"Maybe what?" I asked.

"Maybe we only *thought* we saw it."

Why was Fred backing down? Because he was afraid?

Well, seeing a reflection of something that wasn't in the room was a pretty scary thing. Like out of a horror movie or something.

But I knew I could believe my eyes. I wasn't dreaming and I wasn't imagining it.

I stepped up close to the mirror and gazed down at the bottom. "Buzzy?" I called into the mirror. "Buzzy — are you in there?"

Fred took a step back.

"Buzzy?" I called.

I reached out a hand and touched the glass. It felt surprisingly warm.

I tried to stare deep inside it. But squinting like that only made the reflection blur.

Finally, I turned back to Fred. "Weird, huh?"

"I guess." He crossed the room to the window and stared down at the garage.

"Are you thirsty?" I asked. "I'm going downstairs to get a Coke or something."

"Yeah. I'll take one. Thanks."

As I made my way out of the room, I saw Fred walk back to the mirror. He stopped a few feet in front of it and stared into the glass.

I hurried down to the kitchen and pulled two cans of Coke from the fridge.

When I returned to my room, Fred was gone.

"**H**ey — Fred?"

I searched quickly around my room. Then, still carrying the two Cokes, I went back out to the hall.

"Fred? Are you out here?"

Claudia's door swung open. The music blared out. Some kind of Latin dance music. "What's your problem, Jason?"

"Did you see Fred?"

She frowned at me. "Why would I see Fred? I'm in my room trying to study, aren't I?"

"I know, but —"

"Is this another dumb trick to scare me or something?" she asked.

"No. Really," I said. "Fred was in my room. But now he's gone."

"Try looking in the mirror!" Claudia exclaimed.

35

Then she laughed her hyena laugh and slammed the door.

"Hey, Fred?" I called again.

No reply.

I made my way downstairs. Mom and Dad were in the living room. Dad was down on the floor, shoving a tape into the VCR.

"Did Fred come in here?" I asked. "Did you see him leave?"

They shook their heads.

"We didn't see him," Mom said. "Want to watch a movie with us? We rented an old Hitchcock film."

"I . . . can't," I said. "I've got to find Fred."

"How can you two guys spend all your time playing video games?" Dad asked. "Don't you have any homework?"

"Not tonight," I said.

I walked into the kitchen and picked up the phone from the wall. I punched in Fred's number.

Did he go home?

I listened to it ring. Five times . . . six . . .

I clicked off the phone and put it back on the wall.

"Weird," I muttered.

I made my way back to the living room. My parents were sitting on opposite ends of the couch. They had turned out all the lights. The light from the TV screen flickered over them eerily.

"This is a pretty scary movie," Mom said, turning to me. "It's a real classic. If Fred went home, why don't you come watch it with us?"

"Uh . . . I'm not really in the mood for scary movies," I told her.

I stopped at the bottom of the stairs. "Are we going to leave Buzzy in the garage all night?" I asked.

Dad nodded. "I think we have to, Jason. He's still barking out there. I don't know what got into him. In the morning, your mom and I will make an appointment for him at the vet. Maybe she'll be able to tell us what's wrong."

I climbed the stairs and returned to my room. I half expected to find Fred sitting there, practicing the hockey game.

But no. The room was still empty.

"Fred?" I called weakly.

I dropped down onto the edge of my bed.

And jumped up instantly when I heard a sound from my closet.

I turned to the closed closet door. And heard a cough from inside.

"Fred? Hey, Fred — what's the big idea?"

I pulled open the door — and screamed as the hideous creature leaped out at me.

12

Roaring like an enraged animal, it grabbed me by the shoulders and shoved me back. Its gleaming red eyes glared furiously at me.

Green gobs of drool clung to its jagged rows of yellow teeth.

I staggered back in terror.

It took me only a second or two to realize that it was Claudia wearing that disgusting monster mask she bought for Halloween.

But those two seconds were long enough to give my sister a good laugh.

"AAAAAGH!" I let out a disgusted cry.

Fooled again. *Again!*

She pulled off the rubber mask and tossed it to my bed. She laughed until she had tears in her eyes.

"I don't believe it," I muttered. "I just don't believe it."

I stood there, hands pressed against my waist, breathing hard. Feeling like a total jerk.

"Think you could scream like that again?" Claudia teased. "That was a classic."

"Ha ha," I muttered.

"Tell me something. Is there anything that *doesn't* scare you?" she asked.

She didn't wait for an answer. She grabbed up her mask and headed back to her room. I heard her laughing all the way down the hall.

It isn't funny, I thought.

Not funny at all.

Something strange is going on here. Something *real*. Something frightening.

I stood there in the center of my room, clenching and unclenching my fists.

I felt so angry. Angry at myself.

Finally, I shook my head hard as if shaking all my angry thoughts away.

I got changed for bed.

Before I turned off the lights, I gazed into the new mirror one more time. I studied my reflection. Nothing strange about it. Just me standing there in my pajamas, looking kind of tired, my hair standing up in clumps as usual.

I stared deep into the mirror. It was so clear, as if there were no glass at all. I didn't see anything unusual. My wrestling posters filled the glass, the names in big black type reversed.

I shut off the light, climbed into bed, and pulled the covers up to my chin.

I shut my eyes and thought about Fred.

Maybe I should call his house one more time, I thought.

No. His parents don't like phone calls late at night.

I yawned. I'll see Fred at school in the morning. He'll probably have some simple explanation for why he left without saying good-bye.

I scolded myself for getting so worked up, for letting my imagination run away from me. I felt so angry that I let Claudia scare me again.

Why did I always make it so easy for her?

If only I could stop screaming like a frightened baby, maybe she'd stop trying to terrify me all the time.

I took a deep breath and let it out slowly.

Go to sleep, Jason, I ordered myself. Stop thinking and just go to sleep.

But a sound floated into my mind.

Buzzy . . . barking out in the garage.

Why didn't he stop? Why was he carrying on like that?

What was he barking about?

I covered my ears, but it didn't block out Buzzy's sharp, angry cries.

And then I heard another sound.

A whimpering.

A high, shrill whimpering.

The sound Buzzy always made when he was hurt or frightened.

I heard the furious barking outside and the frightened whimpering from inside.

From *where* inside?

From the mirror?

The next morning, I had gym class first period. I dropped my backpack in my locker and headed to the gym to get changed for soccer.

"Hey —" I called out when I saw Fred at the other end of the locker room. He already had on his shorts and T-shirt and was lacing up his shoes.

I slammed my gym locker and pushed my way through the crowded aisle to him. "Fred — what's up?"

He shrugged.

In gym shorts and a sleeveless T-shirt, he really looks like a lanky skeleton. I must weigh more than he does, and I'm at least a head shorter!

"Where'd you go last night?" I asked. "I went back to my room, and you were gone."

"Uh . . . yeah . . . well . . ." He squinted at me as if trying to remember. "I had to get home, Jason. I forgot I had something to do."

I frowned at him. "You could have said good-bye or something. I searched all over for you. I was kind of worried."

"Sorry," Fred said, and shrugged his bony shoulders again.

We both turned when we heard the coach's whistle. "Let's go, guys," the coach growled. "It's warm out, so we're outside today. Try to get a game in before the rain starts again. The field is already a little muddy, so be careful, okay?"

We trooped out of the locker room to the field beyond the middle-school playground. It was a humid gray day with big storm clouds low overhead.

It had rained during the night and the field was soft, with wide mud patches dotting the grass. A strong wind blew raindrops down on us from the trees.

I shivered as I took my place. We already had our teams, so we all knew where to go.

I played forward. I turned back and looked for Fred, who was on my team. He hated soccer and always tried to hide in a back corner somewhere so he wouldn't have to kick the ball much.

I didn't see him in his usual place.

The whistle blew to start the game.

I was so surprised to see Fred come out dribbling the ball, I nearly fell over.

He gave it short kicks, keeping it close in front of him as he crossed the field.

He's going to trip over the ball and go flying into the mud, I thought. Why is he doing this?

To my surprise, Fred didn't trip. Instead, he sent a perfect pass to Robby McIntire, a teammate. Robby dodged a defender, brought the ball close to the goal, and went for a shot.

The goalie deflected the ball with his shoulder.

To my shock, Fred was there to retrieve it. He kicked it furiously — and sent it deep into the net for a goal!

His teammates cheered and clapped Fred on the back and slapped him high fives.

"Way to go!" I called to him. I slapped him a high five. He slapped me back so hard, he nearly threw my arm out of joint.

"Hey!" I cried out.

But Fred was already back in position.

"Wow. He must have had a *big* bowl of Wheaties this morning!" I told myself.

Then the game got even more surprising.

I mean, Fred was the surprising part.

He was *everywhere*.

Wherever the ball bounced, there was Fred.

He powered it down the field. He kicked goals from a mile away.

He shouted and waved his arms and cheered his

teammates on. He elbowed players out of his way. He shouldered guys into the mud, then trampled over them.

Fred took over the game, bullying everyone, challenging anyone to stop him. He dominated. *Dominated!*

I never saw anything like it. Skinny, wimpy Fred, who couldn't handle a video soccer game. Wiping up the field with everyone, smashing the other team, kicking furious goal after goal.

When Coach Simmons blew his whistle to end the game, I went running over to Fred. Fred's shorts and T-shirt were covered in thick mud. He had been in every battle of the game, had thrown himself into every play.

I broke through the circle of cheering guys around him. "Fred!" I shouted. "You were amazing, man. You were possessed! Totally *possessed!*"

To my shock, his smile faded. His eyes flared angrily.

He lurched forward, shoved guys out of the way, and grabbed the front of my shirt. Pulled it so hard, he nearly lifted me off the ground.

"Huh?" I uttered.

"What did you say?" Fred bellowed.

"I . . . uh . . . said you were possessed. What's the big deal?"

"Don't . . . ever . . . say . . . that!" Fred growled.

And with an angry cry, he leaped onto me. Knocked me to the ground.

45

I landed hard on my back and felt the air whoosh from my lungs.

As I struggled to breathe, Fred jumped onto my chest.

"Owww . . . my ribs!" I groaned.

I couldn't squirm free. I couldn't breathe.

He raised his fists and started pounding me, punching me furiously.

His normally pale face was bright red. In a rage, he punched me, punched hard, harder.

Each blow sent a stab of pain down my body.

"Get off! Get *off*!" I pleaded.

I actually saw stars, bright white and shimmery stars.

I felt blood flow from my nose.

"Fred — stop! Stop! Please!"

14

"**Y**ou look as if you've been in a car wreck," Mrs. Johnson, the school nurse, said, shaking her head.

I groaned in reply.

"I thought you and Fred were best friends," she said.

"We were," I whispered.

She dabbed my cut eyebrow with cotton dipped in alcohol. "It took two teachers to pry him off you, Jason."

"Tell me about it." I sighed.

"You're lucky you don't have broken ribs," Mrs. Johnson said, pulling bandages from the supply closet.

"Yeah. I'm lucky," I moaned.

"What set him off like that?" she asked. "It's like he just exploded."

I shrugged, then instantly regretted it. Shrugging made my whole body ache.

"He was possessed out there," I said. "Fred hates soccer. He's terrible at it. He's terrible at all sports. But today . . ."

She pressed a bandage over my forehead.

"Well, he's been suspended," she said. "His parents have to come in to see Mr. Royal this afternoon. Does that make you feel any better?"

"No," I replied. "He's my friend. At least, I *think* he is."

Mrs. Johnson sent me home to rest up. I walked in through the kitchen door and glanced at the clock over the stove. Only eleven-thirty in the morning.

"Anyone home?" I called weakly.

Of course not. Why would anyone be home?

Claudia was in school. Mom was at work. Dad was starting his new job today.

What am I going to do all day? I asked myself.

Normally, I'd be jumping up and down with joy. But now, just the *thought* of jumping up and down sent shivers of pain down my back!

I didn't feel hungry. Actually, I felt really sick to my stomach. Having someone punch you in the guts with all his might can make you feel a little queasy.

But I pulled open the refrigerator and peered

inside. I spotted some fried chicken pieces wrapped in Saran Wrap, left over from last night.

Good, I thought.

If I do get hungry later, I'll have something for lunch.

It was kind of creepy being home during a school day, when no one else was around. The hum of the refrigerator seemed so loud. Every step I took made the floor creak. I could hear the clock ticking in the living room.

"Get plenty of rest," Mrs. Johnson had said.

I decided to go up to my room, get a book to read, then settle down on the living room couch with it.

My stomach and chest throbbed with pain as I climbed the stairs. Maybe I *did* break a rib, I thought, groaning.

Once again, I pictured Fred. Fred my friend, leaping on top of me in a total rage. Pounding me with his fists. His face so red and angry. Pounding me ...

Pounding me ...

Just thinking about it made my stomach heave. I pressed my hand over my mouth as I started to gag.

No ... No ... .

I stopped and held my breath until I felt better.

I swallowed hard. I had such a bitter taste in my mouth.

I wiped cold sweat off my forehead with the back of my hand. "Ow!" I forgot about the bandage up there.

I took another deep breath. Then I started across my room to the bookshelf on the far wall.

I didn't plan to look in the mirror.

I planned to walk right past it.

But something caught my eye, and I turned.

Turned in time to see something move.

Yes!

I didn't imagine it.

Something moved — *inside the mirror!*

froze.

The cut on my forehead throbbed.

I squinted through the pain, squinted into the mirror.

Rain pelted my bedroom window, making a loud drumming sound. The low storm clouds made the morning sky an eerie yellow-black.

I hadn't turned on a lamp. The gray light from the window cast long shadows over my bed, the old dresser, and my carpet.

The shadows shifted and slid over the face of the mirror.

I squinted at my reflection in the glass. Behind me, I could see my bed and the wrestling posters on the wall.

But everything was dark, dark and shadowy, as if a gray curtain had been pulled over the glass.

The reflection seemed gloomier than the room, darker and colder.

Maybe I'm imagining that, I thought.

But then I saw the charcoal black shadows shift in the glass. Like black clouds, they puffed and rolled over each other.

Yes.

Something moving in the glass.

I turned and glanced behind me. The room stood in perfect stillness.

But in the glass, in the murky, dark glass, the shadows were dancing, rolling. Moving closer . . .

I watched in openmouthed silence as the shadows split in two. Formed two misty figures. A tall figure and a short dot of a figure.

A dog?

Buzzy?

A shadow Buzzy?

And why did the other figure, the tall, lean one, why did it remind me of Fred?

Was it the narrow, rounded head? The slender, bony shoulders?

His posture? The way the faceless, cloudy figure stood hunched with its head hanging down?

Was I really staring at shadow figures of Fred and Buzzy?

Or was I totally losing it? Letting my imagination go crazy? Letting my fear make a fool of me once again?

Wind howled outside the window. At least, I *thought* the howling came from outside.

Rain drummed on the glass and the window ledge.

The room grew even darker.

The figures in the mirror faded.

I shoved my cold hands deep into my pockets.

I didn't move. I squinted into the mirror.

Dark now. Dark as night.

The figures had vanished.

I stared at smooth, dark glass.

And trembled. Trembled until my teeth chattered.

I'm afraid, I realized.

I'm afraid of my own bedroom.

There's *something* inside this mirror.

What am I going to do? Who will believe me?

What does it want?

What?

16

That night, it took me hours to get to sleep.

I didn't want to sleep in my room. But I couldn't let Mom, Dad, and Claudia know that I was scared.

I kept picturing Buzzy, snarling so furiously with his teeth bared. Attacking me, biting and clawing.

What happened to the poor dog? He had always been so quiet and calm and gentle.

Dad said he didn't know how long we could keep Buzzy in the garage. The neighbors were complaining about his constant barking and howling.

Tossing and turning in bed, I wondered if Buzzy would ever be normal again.

I thought about Fred too.

We'd been friends since first grade, and we'd never had a serious argument.

Why did he attack me like that?

I told him he was possessed during the soccer game. I meant it as a compliment. So why did he get so angry? Why did he go berserk and totally lose it?

It was all such a mystery. How did he suddenly get so good at soccer? He wasn't just good. He was *amazing*! And he was so tough, so confident, so aggressive.

Fred had always been the worst player in gym class. This morning, it was like he was a different person.

Now he was suspended from school. I thought maybe he'd call me tonight to apologize. Or at least explain.

But the phone didn't ring.

I glanced at my clock radio. Twelve-fifteen. I felt really tired and wide awake at the same time. I had so many puzzling questions. Millions of questions — but no answers.

I shut my eyes and tried not to think.

I pictured a blue sky. Fluffy white clouds. The clouds floated past, one by one. One cloud ... two ... three ...

I was just drifting off to sleep when I heard the sound.

A dog barking?

I sat straight up, wide awake again and very alert.

I held my breath and listened hard.

Another high dog bark, softer this time, far away.

Not Buzzy, I decided. The sound is too far away. It must be a dog down the block.

I settled my head back on the pillow.

But another sound made me sit right back up.

I tilted my head toward it, listening.

Soft breathing?

Yes. Steady, soft breathing.

From my closet, I guessed, squinting across my dark bedroom.

I didn't panic. I knew it had to be Claudia.

Claudia hiding all this time in my closet, waiting for the right moment to leap out and scare me.

Why didn't she give up? Why was it so important to her to frighten me all the time?

Maybe I'll give *her* a scare this time, I decided.

I lowered my feet to the carpet and silently stood up.

The soft, steady breathing grew louder as I crept across the room toward the closet.

I stuck out my hand, preparing to grab the knob and jerk the closet door open.

But halfway across the room, I stopped — and gasped in horror — when I realized . . .

. . . Realized the breathing didn't come from the closet.

It came from the *mirror*.

stood frozen in the middle of my room. I stared straight ahead at the closet door.

I didn't dare turn to look at the mirror.

But I could hear the steady breaths at my side . . .

"*Hunnnnh . . . hunnnnh . . . hunnnnnh . . .*"

I shut my eyes tightly, as if trying to shut out the terrifying sound. My hands suddenly felt cold and wet. I wiped them on my pajama bottoms. Chill after chill swept down my back.

"*Hunnnnh . . . hunnnnh . . . hunnnnnh . . .*"

I opened my eyes. The room suddenly seemed so dark. No light at all came through the window.

With a lurching movement, I forced myself to the wall and clicked on the ceiling light.

That's better, I thought, blinking as my eyes adjusted to the light. Now — maybe — I can face the mirror. . . .

"Hunnnnh . . . hunnnnh . . . hunnnnnh . . ."

The steady breathing filled my ears. My heart raced wildly.

I took a step away from the wall. Then another.

I kept my eyes down until I was directly in front of the mirror.

Then, with the breathing sounds so close, so close . . . I turned slowly and gazed into the glass.

18

"**H**uh?" I let out a startled cry.

My bedroom was bright now under the yellow glow of the ceiling light.

But the mirror was dark. Dark as if no light were on.

I stared into the glass. Black as night.

Not reflecting. Not reflecting anything. A solid sheet of black.

"No. It's ... *impossible*," I whispered.

Swallowing hard, I took a step forward.

And listened to the breathing. Definitely from inside the mirror.

"*Hunnnnh ... hunnnnh ...*"

Each breath made my heart skip. Each breath sent a shiver down my body.

"Who are you?" I called out in a tiny voice. "Where are you?"

"Hunnnh . . . hunnnh . . ."

And then the blackness in the glass faded to a gray mist. I watched as the gray mist shifted and floated over the glass, floated like a cloud.

I stood staring, not blinking, not breathing. I pressed my cold, trembling hands against the sides of my pajamas.

And I gaped in horror as it formed a figure. A human figure.

Then the cloud began to stretch — stretch until it was long and tall, taller than me.

A narrow head took shape on top of a slender body.

What's happening? I wondered. What am I watching?

I wanted to turn and run. I wanted to scream.

But the terrifying sight held me in place.

I didn't even cry out when the cloudy form became sharper and the face brightened.

And I recognized Fred.

Yes. Fred's face on the cloudy gray body.

Fred inside the mirror. His eyes so cold and dead. Not blue anymore. A ghostly gray.

His expression pleading. His mouth open in a silent cry.

"Hunnnnh . . . hunnnh . . ."

Fred, breathing so softly inside the dark glass, his face so sad, so unbearably sad . . .

And then he raised his skinny hands. Raised his palms to the glass as if trying to push out.

60

"Jason — help me."

His voice a whisper from inside the misty mirror. His dull eyes pleading.

"Jason — help me. Help me out of here!"

"Fred?" I whispered. "Can you hear me? Can you see me?"

His open hands spread over the glass. He stared out at me, shimmering, a cloud, just a cloud.

"Help meeeeee."

And then his hands shot out from inside the mirror.

No sound. No shattering glass.

Fred's hands burst out from inside the mirror — and grabbed my hands.

And began to pull. Pull me to the glass.

"No!" I screamed. "Let go! Let go of me!"

19

"**L**et go! Let go!"

His hands were so cold, colder than any hands I'd ever touched. His hard fingers tightened around my wrists. He pulled . . . pulled with incredible strength.

"Fred — let go!" I screamed again.

I felt my heart pound against my chest. Felt the blood throb at my temples. Saw Fred's gray eyes narrow as he pulled me closer . . . closer . . .

And the blackness of the mirror seemed to pour out into the bedroom. It poured over me, covering me, shutting out all light.

And I sank into it.

Sank into complete darkness. A deep, cold blackness all around.

*　　*　　*

I opened my eyes. Blinked. Blinked against the bright light from the ceiling.

I raised my head groggily. My mouth felt dry. My left arm had fallen asleep.

I blinked a few more times. And realized I was on my bedroom floor. I sat up slowly.

Had I fallen asleep on the floor?

Had I dreamed the horrifying scene with Fred grabbing me from inside the mirror?

All a nightmare?

I raised my hands close and studied them. I gaped at the red scratches on my wrists. Scrape marks from where Fred had grabbed me.

Not a dream.

It had happened. Fred's pleading face. His hands shooting out from behind the glass. The darkness floating over my room. Fred pulling me, pulling me to the mirror.

But then, how did I end up on the floor?

I turned unsteadily to the mirror. The glass was solid black once again.

The bright light beamed down from the ceiling. But the mirror didn't reflect my room.

It didn't reflect anything. It stood in front of the wall, a dark hole, a black tunnel, leading ... where?

I climbed to my feet, brushing back my hair with both hands. I kept my eyes on the glass.

I've got to get Mom and Dad, I decided. I've got

to show them the black glass. Then maybe they'll finally believe that something weird is going on.

They'll say you were dreaming, I thought.

I shook my head hard. *No. You'll MAKE them believe you!*

I took a step to the door. But stopped when the glass began to change again.

Another gray cloud formed. Another misty figure, looming forward from the deep blackness.

The gray mist swirled like a tornado of smoke, tumbling over itself, pulsing, bubbling.

A head formed on a human body. Covered in gray, covered like a cocoon.

And then the smoke drifted away, and I could see the figure's face clearly.

So clearly.

My mouth dropped open, but no sound came out.

And I stared at the face in horror.

My face!

My face inside the glass, staring back at me with such sad, dark eyes.

I took a staggering step back from the mirror. Nearly tripped over my own bare feet.

"N-no —" I whispered.

I pressed my hands against my cheeks. I couldn't stop my legs from trembling.

"Who are you?" I asked in a tiny, trembling voice. "How . . . how is this happening?"

The dark eyes studied me through the glass. The lips moved before the sound reached me.

"Jason — I am your ghost!"

"No!" I screamed. "No! You can't be!"

"Yes. I am your ghost."

"But ... but ... if you're my ghost, does that mean I *died*?"

20

I stared at my face in the dark glass. My eyes, my wild hair, my mouth. The mouth curled up in a cold grin. "Yes, Jason. You died."

"No!" I screamed. "I'm standing here! I'm staring at you. I'm alive! I'm *alive!*"

The face in the mirror didn't reply. The cold grin froze on his shadowy face.

"You're lying!" I accused. "You're lying — right?"

"You died, Jason," the figure repeated. "That's why I am here. I am your ghost."

"When did I die?" I yelled. "Tell me! If I'm dead, when did I die?"

The ghost shut his eyes. "Tonight," he whispered.

My breath caught in my throat.

I stared at the grinning face. "How did I die?" I finally choked out.

"You died of fright, Jason."

I clenched and unclenched my fists. I held my breath to stop my trembling.

That's a lie, I decided.

I'm not dead. I'm standing here in my room.

I'm staring into the mirror at . . . at . . .

. . . My own ghost?

The ghost raised a hand and motioned for me to come closer. "Come in, Jason," he whispered. "Come join me."

"No way!" I cried.

I watched his hand — *my* hand — waving me in. Waving slowly, steadily.

"Come join me, Jason. You will be safe in here."

"Safe?" I asked. "With you?"

"I *am* you!" the ghost declared. "Of course you will be safe with me. Come in. Come in." The hand waving, waving so hypnotically.

I felt myself drawn to him, drawn to the mirror, as if he were tugging me forward.

"Come in, Jason. Come in."

I took a step closer.

I couldn't resist.

The hand waved . . . waved slowly . . . motioning to me. Guiding me in.

I took another step. I couldn't feel the carpet beneath my feet. I felt dazed, as if I were sleep-walking.

"Walk right through the glass?" I asked in a tiny voice.

"Come in, Jason. You will be safe in here with me, Jason," the ghost whispered.

"Yes," I whispered back. "Yes."

I took another step. I suddenly felt so light.

I'm floating, I thought.

Floating into a dream.

Then I felt the ghost's hands grip my shoulders. And pull.

I'm going in, I realized.

I'm going into the mirror.

21

The sharp bark of a dog stopped me.

I leaned into the blackness — and saw Buzzy, a dim, tiny dot in the distance.

He barked shrilly, as if warning me away.

The ghost's hands tightened on my shoulders. He pulled harder.

"No —" I protested, squinting at Buzzy's dim outline, listening to his sharp squeals and barks.

And beside the dog, stepping from the deep blackness, I saw the thin gray figure again. Fred!

He called to me, his voice faint as if from a hundred miles away. "Jason, don't come. Don't come in!"

His words snapped me from my spell.

With a furious cry, I jerked myself free of the ghost's hard grip.

I stumbled back, struggling to keep my balance.

But I fell.

And landed on my back on the bedroom carpet.

Scrambling to my feet, I raised my eyes to the mirror. And saw me — saw my ghost — open his mouth in an angry roar.

"I ordered you to come in here!" he bellowed.

As he screamed, his mouth opened wider, wider. Then it flapped back over his head until it appeared to swallow his face!

I stared in sickened horror as my face disappeared, and his whole head turned inside out.

And now I was gaping at the head of a hideous monster! A fat red tongue flopped out from the creature's pale wet skin. A red nose, bulbous with three nostrils, flapped loose from its face. The eyes were yellow, the size of tennis balls, and bulged out from deep red sockets.

"Noooooooo." I uttered a moan of horror and shrank back.

The creature's body changed slowly. Expanding in all directions, turning into a hard, purple shell.

The arms — *my* arms — slid into the monster's shiny wet skin. And enormous red claws poked out. Like giant crab claws, they stretched and clicked, clicked as if sharpening themselves.

The whole creature glistened with sweat. The yellow tennis ball eyes rolled like fly eyes in the round red face. The crab claws raised themselves up from the purple hard-shelled body, clicking, snapping and clicking.

I watched in stunned horror, my fright changing to anger. "You lied!" I yelled, shaking my fist at the hideous creature in the mirror. "You lied to me! You're not my ghost! You're a *monster*!"

The creature's eyes bulged wider. The mouth opened, revealing two jagged rows of purple teeth. The fat red tongue snapped from side to side.

Then it raised its giant crab claws. Held them up and opened them wide.

The mirror seemed to part as a claw shot out into the room, slapped the side of my head, then tightened around my throat.

22

Choking, I reached up and grabbed the claw with both hands.

I tried to pry it open, but the hard shell was slippery and wet.

My hands slid right off.

The claw tightened around my neck and pulled me toward the mirror.

I pounded the claw frantically with my fists. I twisted and squirmed. I leaned my body back, shot my feet up, and tried to kick at it.

No. The monster was too strong.

One claw slapped at my head. The other claw gripped my neck and pulled me up.

I felt my feet leave the floor.

The creature was lifting me into the air. Lifting me and carrying me into the mirror.

I stared up into the monster's ugly red face. The yellow eyes spun wildly. The enormous mouth hung open in an excited grin.

I couldn't breathe. My chest ached and throbbed. My hands thrashed in the air wildly.

The claw lifted me higher, into the mirror. I could feel icy coldness on my face. See the darkness behind the glass sweep over me.

As the creature pulled me beside him, my hand bumped the dresser. I tried to grab onto the dresser top. Something to hold to keep me in the room.

My hand slapped the wood. My fingers wrapped around something.

I couldn't tell what it was.

The claw opened, slid off my throat.

I landed in darkness.

The creature rose up in front of me.

So cold in here. And so dark. I'm inside the mirror, I realized.

The monster leaned over me. I raised my hands to protect myself — and saw what I had picked up from the dresser.

A small hand mirror.

Not much of a weapon.

But it was all I had.

The monster leaned down, opening its hideous mouth, wider, wider, as if to swallow me the way it had swallowed its own head.

And as its hot, sour breath swam over me, I gripped the handle of the mirror, pulled back my arm ...

... And slammed the mirror as hard as I could into the shell over the monster's belly.

I stood frozen for a second. Waiting. Watching.

Nothing happened.

It didn't even seem to notice.

23

"Let me out!" I screamed. "Let me out of here!"

My cry rang through the eerie darkness. Echo after echo, fading into the distance, repeating my horror.

I began pounding the mirror against the creature's body. Pounding frantically. Batting him with it. Holding the handle with both hands and swinging with all my strength.

My blows did no harm.

The creature raised his giant claws and snapped them in a steady rhythm, as if celebrating his triumph.

Its fat lips smacked each other wetly and then opened in a growl of words: *"Welcome to your new...home. I'll be taking your place... outside..."*

"Nooo!" I screamed again, flailing at the grinning creature with the hand mirror.

And then the mirror slipped from my hand.

I made a wild grab for it.

Caught it.

It spun in my hand.

The little round mirror reflected the glass of the big mirror.

I saw the monster's reflection in the little mirror.

And then, as it bounced off the bigger sheet of glass, I saw *two* monsters reflected.

Then four.

Then a dozen.

A dozen crablike monsters, claws raised above their heads.

Startled, I struggled to hold the mirror steady.

The dozen monster reflections became two dozen. Then more, more monsters, growing smaller, smaller, stretching into infinity.

Staring into the glass, it took me a few seconds to realize that the reflections had become real!

There were hundreds of monsters in the mirror now.

All roaring, snapping their ugly wet claws, lumbering forward . . .

. . . Moving forward to attack me!

24

I staggered back as the creatures stampeded. Their feet thundered as they moved to attack. The crack of their snapping claws sounded like trees breaking.

I pressed my hands over my ears. But I couldn't shut out the deafening clatter, the echoing roars of fury.

I took another step back as the creatures rose over me. Hundreds of raised claws snapped and gouged the air.

What have I done?

The horrifying question flashed through my mind as I backed up . . .

. . . And fell.

. . . Fell out of the big mirror.

I landed on my back on the bedroom floor. I felt too weak to stand up. Stretched out on the carpet, hands still pressed tightly over my ears to drown out the furious sound, I watched in amazement as the monsters attacked *each other*.

Claws ripped away claws. Tennis ball eyes were pulled from their sockets. The eyes bounced and flew across the mirror.

Creatures tossed back their hideous heads in wails of pain.

I gaped in stunned silence as monsters swallowed each other, clawed away skin and insides, tore at each other, roaring and snarling.

Then I forced myself to look away. Forced myself to stand up on my shaking legs. Forced myself to breathe.

My whole body shuddering, I spun away from the mirror.

And staggered to the hall.

"Mom! Dad! Please! Come quick!"

I lurched down the dark hall to their room, screaming my head off, my voice high and quivering in panic.

"Please! Hurry!"

My screams brought them from their bedroom, yawning, blinking away sleep.

"Jason — what's wrong?" Dad asked. "A nightmare or something?"

"Just hurry!" I grabbed his hand and pulled. I tugged him into my room. Mom hurried close behind, tightening the belt on her robe.

I pulled them up to the mirror. "Look! It — it's unbelievable!"

All three of us stared into the mirror.

At the reflection of my room. The desk. My wrestling posters on the wall.

No battling monsters. No flying claws and eyeballs.

"I'm not crazy! I'm not crazy!" I screamed without even realizing it.

Mom rested her hands on my shoulders. Dad narrowed his eyes at me, his face lined with concern.

I jerked free of Mom's hands. "I'll prove it to you! Watch. I'm not crazy! Just watch!"

"Jason — please," Dad said softly.

"What are you going to do? What do you want to prove to us?" Mom whispered.

"Just watch," I said. "I'm going in. I'm going into the mirror. Watch me!"

I had to show them. I had to show them that I wasn't crazy.

I lowered my shoulder and plunged into the glass.

25

"**O**w!"

My shoulder hit the solid mirror hard. Pain shot down my arm. I stumbled back.

"Jason, please —" Mom pulled me away gently.

"Why are you so frightened of the mirror?" Dad asked.

"There are — there are *monsters* living inside it!"

Still holding on to me, Mom turned to Dad. "Maybe we should get rid of it. It's given him nightmares ever since we bought it."

Dad rubbed his stubbly beard. "But we have to show him that there aren't any monsters in there."

"Stop talking about me as if I'm not here!" I screamed, clenching my fists. "I'm standing right here! And I'm not crazy! I saw monsters in the

80

mirror. They pulled me inside. It's dark in there. And cold. I think I saw Fred and Buzzy in there too."

"Fred and Buzzy?" Mom spread her hand over my forehead, testing to see if I had a fever.

Dad's frown grew deeper. "You saw Fred and Buzzy in the mirror?" He turned to Mom again. "Should we call Dr. Fleeson?"

"He doesn't have a temperature," Mom said. "I — I don't know what to say."

"Sometimes nightmares can seem very real," Dad told me.

I opened my mouth to argue. But I could see there was no way they'd ever believe me.

I let out a weary, defeated sigh. "Forget it. Let's go back to bed."

The next morning, I got dressed quickly with my back to the mirror. I tried not to look into it. But I couldn't help myself. I took a few quick glances.

The reflection was totally normal. Morning sunlight from my bedroom window washed over the glass.

No creatures pretending to be my ghost. No figures calling to me to come save them.

I shivered, thinking of the night before.

"It wasn't a nightmare," I whispered to myself.

I grabbed the hand mirror off my dresser and shoved it into my pocket. Somehow having it made me feel safer. Then I hurried downstairs to breakfast.

Mom and Dad greeted me with searching stares. I guessed they were studying me, trying to see if I was still crazy.

Claudia sat at the kitchen table, dressed for school, shoving a banana into her mouth like a chimpanzee.

She opened her mouth wide to show me the mashed-up goo stuck to her braces.

"Thanks for sharing that," I muttered.

"I hear you totally freaked last night," Claudia said, grinning.

"Claudia!" Mom cried sharply. "We weren't going to talk about it — remember?"

"Maybe the little boy needs a night-light," Claudia said nastily.

"That's enough!" Dad snapped. "Finish your cereal. You're going to be late."

"Let's try to be a little nicer around here," Mom said, frowning at Claudia.

"How can you be nice to a nut?" Claudia replied. She chugged down her orange juice and jumped up from the table. "Bye." She disappeared into the front hall.

"I want you to walk Jason to school," Dad called after her.

"I don't want to go with Claudia. I'm riding my bike," I told him. I sipped my orange juice.

"Do you feel better?" Mom asked.

I shrugged. "I guess. I didn't get much sleep."

"Do you want to see the doctor?"

"I'm not sick!" I insisted.

"We can take out the mirror," Dad said, tugging at the knot on his tie. "If it really is bothering you."

I didn't know how to answer. I wanted that frightening mirror *out* of my room.

But I didn't want them to remove it until I proved to them that I wasn't crazy. That something really terrifying was going on inside it.

"Let's talk about it this weekend," Mom said, carrying dishes to the sink. "We don't have time now. We're all going to be late."

I gulped down the rest of my cereal, glad I didn't have to decide about the mirror. Then I packed up my backpack, pulled on a jacket, and hurried out the back door to get my bike.

"Oh, nooo!" A cry escaped my throat as I stopped short in the driveway. And stared in shock at the garage.

At the huge, jagged chunk ripped out of the bottom of the garage door.

"Buzzy?" I cried. "Buzzy? Are you still in there?"

26

The wood had been shattered, as if someone had punched a big hole in the door from inside the garage. Chunks of broken wood lay strewn over the driveway.

"Buzzy?"

I bent down, grabbed the handle, and pulled up the door.

My eyes searched the garage.

What a mess!

Garden tools tossed over the concrete floor. My bike on its side. A big bag of planting soil ripped open, the black dirt spread over the floor. The lawn mower turned upside down.

"Buzzy?"

No sign of him.

I scratched my head. "Did Buzzy *do* all this?"

Did the little dog wreck the garage? Then chew or claw his way out the door?

No. Impossible, I decided.

Buzzy was too small. The wood of the garage door was at least two inches thick!

Mom and Dad had already left for work. I couldn't tell them about this mess until later.

Where did Buzzy go? I hoped he was okay.

I grabbed the handlebars and pulled my bike up. I brushed planting soil off the seat and frame. Then I climbed on, took one last glance at the garage, and pedaled down the driveway.

I stood up and pedaled hard. The cool morning air felt good on my burning cheeks.

I headed up the block toward Fred's house. The two of us usually rode to school together. But as his house came into view, I remembered that Fred was suspended.

Lucky guy, I thought.

He probably gets to sleep late!

I gazed up at his house — and nearly fell off my bike.

I hit the hand brakes hard. The bike squealed to a sharp stop. I had to grab the handlebars to keep from being thrown over the front of the bike.

"Oh, wow."

I stared at the broken windows on the front of Fred's house. All of the downstairs windows had been shattered. Big shards of glass reflected the sunlight on the grass. I saw jagged glass on the front stoop where the storm door had been smashed.

What is going on here?

My heart started to pound. I gripped the handlebars tighter to keep from toppling over.

The front door stood wide open. The inside of the house was dark.

"Fred?" I called.

I pedaled up Fred's driveway.

"Fred? Are you in there? What's going on?"

I was halfway up the drive when I glimpsed a figure at the corner of the block.

A tall, thin figure, short blond hair gleaming in the sun.

"Fred!"

I jumped off my bike. It crashed noisily to the driveway.

Fred stood in the middle of the street, arms raised high — *holding a car over his head!*

27

"Fred —?"

I started running down the street to him, waving wildly.

"Fred? What are you doing?"

I stopped when I heard screams. I saw people inside the car. As Fred balanced the car over his head, the people inside were pounding the windows, screaming their heads off.

"Fred! Put it down!" I yelled. I took a few running steps toward him. "Fred — set it down! You'll get in trouble. You'll get in horrible trouble!"

Above his head, the car rocked in his hands. The people inside shrieked and slapped the windows.

Fred turned quickly. An angry growl escaped his throat.

"Fred — put it down! Listen to me!"

He pulled the car back . . . back . . .

"Noooo!" I let out a scream when I realized what he planned to do. He planned to *heave* it at me!

"Noooo!" One more shout, cut off in horror when I saw Fred's eyes, bright yellow eyes — demon eyes — glowing brighter than a traffic light.

It's not Fred, I realized, shrinking back in horror.

The eyes glowed brighter, so bright I had to turn away.

It's not Fred — it's some kind of monster!

Fred tossed back his head and roared. The muscles in his arms bulged.

The car rocked above him. The people inside screamed and pleaded, pounding their fists.

I backed away quickly. Then I turned and started to run.

I heard the wail of sirens. I heard angry shouts from the neighbors' houses. Saw people staring in disbelief from their front doors.

It's not Fred, I told myself. It's not really Fred.

I grabbed my bike and hopped on to it.

Four black-and-white squad cars squealed to a stop. Police with their guns raised leaped from the cars.

I rode away. I couldn't bear to watch.

It's not really Fred. . . .

A million thoughts whirred through my frantic

brain as I pedaled to school. I pictured the smashed garage door. And the shattered windows in the front of Fred's house.

Buzzy attacked me . . . Fred attacked me too.

But these were monsters . . . monsters that had escaped from the mirror?

Where were the *real* Buzzy and Fred?

Were they trapped inside the mirror? Trapped in that cold, dark world?

It was crazy . . . totally crazy. Who would believe an insane story like that?

The broken door? The smashed windows? A boy strong enough to hold a car over his head?

Even with all that proof, no one would ever believe that the real Fred and Buzzy were trapped in that other world.

I parked my bike in the bike rack. I made my way into school.

But I knew I'd never hear a word anyone said.

I knew I'd be thinking about only one thing all day.

Because I knew what I had to do. I had no choice.

I had to rescue the real Buzzy and Fred.

I had to bring them back.

I had to go inside the mirror one more time.

28

That night, I couldn't eat dinner. My stomach was clenched into a tight knot. My throat was too dry to swallow.

I made an excuse to go up to bed early.

I turned on all the lights in my room. Then I sat down on the edge of the bed and stared into the mirror.

It reflected my room clearly. Like a normal mirror.

But I knew if I waited patiently, it would change. I propped my head in my hands and stared straight ahead.

After a few minutes, the light in the mirror dimmed.

The glass clouded over.

Inside the mirror, my room faded away, replaced by a gloomy blackness and swirls of gray mist.

"Here goes, Jason," I whispered.

I pushed myself to my feet and took a few hesitant steps across the room.

I was just a few feet from the mirror when I heard the voice calling to me faintly, as if from far away. "Help me, Jason. Please, come help me."

"I'm coming!" I shouted into the mirror.

But my legs began to tremble so hard, I couldn't take another step. My heart pounded in my chest. I suddenly felt breathless and dizzy.

"Help me, Jason. Please — hurry!"

Even so faint and distant, I recognized Fred's voice. And the sound forced me to move.

I stepped up to the dark glass and leaned my head inside. Cold, heavy air rushed over me. I shivered.

Squinting through the swirling mist, I searched for the crab-clawed monster.

No sign of him.

Was he destroyed for good in that battle of monsters?

I cupped my hands around my mouth and called out to the darkness. "Fred? Fred?" My voice hung heavily in the damp fog.

No reply.

I plunged my shoulder into the deep blackness and took a step forward.

The fog surrounded me. The cold air stung my skin and shocked my lungs.

I'm inside, I realized.

I'm inside the mirror.

Shivering from the cold, I took one step. Then another.

The mist clung to my skin. My clothes were wet. My legs felt heavy as I tried to walk through the thick murk.

"Fred? Can you hear me?"

No reply. Only silence, a silence so deep I could hear the blood pulsing at my temples.

I peered into the darkness, waiting for my eyes to adjust.

But there was nothing to see through the curtain of gray mist. Only more gray mist.

I took another cautious step.

"Fred?"

My mouth was still open when I felt the invisible floor give way.

I felt as if I had stepped off a cliff.

My hands shot up. My scream choked in my throat.

I dropped straight down.

The cold air slapped my face, blew my hair wildly, made my shirt flap up.

How far would I fall?

Would I ever land?

No time to think.

I landed hard on my feet.

My ankles cracked. Pain shot up my legs.

I shut my eyes and collapsed to my knees.

And finally . . . finally, my scream escaped my throat.

"AAAAAIIIIIII!"

My shrill wail of horror rang through the lifting darkness.

And when the scream finally ended, and I opened my eyes, I stared at a dozen reflections of myself.

Mirrors. Mirrors all around me.

My shocked, frightened face staring at me from all sides.

I gaped at myself, still shaking, still dizzy from falling.

Where am I? How far did I fall?

Before I could clear my head and stand up, I heard a cry. A cry from close behind me.

And someone grabbed me.

29

I spun around. "Fred!"

He grinned at me, his blue eyes flashing. "It took you long enough."

"Fred — hey!" I cried happily. "I don't believe it!" I slapped him a high five.

We both started laughing, crazy laughing, more out of relief than happiness.

"Where are we?" I asked when we finally stopped.

Fred shrugged. "It's like a hall of mirrors here. Like a fun house or something." He shivered. "Only it isn't any fun."

I heard a sharp *yip*.

I turned and saw Buzzy running toward me, his stubby tail whipping back and forth.

"Buzzy — it's you!" I dropped to my knees and gathered the little guy up in my arms. I brought him close and he licked my nose and face frantically, whimpering.

When the little guy finally calmed down, I stood up and turned back to Fred. "How did this happen? How did you get in here? Do you know the way out?"

He shook his head. "I — I don't know. Buzzy and I — we're trapped in here!"

I spun around, watching our reflections spin with me. Mirrors on all sides.

"I was standing in your room," Fred explained. "Something pulled me in. A creature. It made itself look like me. Then it stepped out of the mirror. I tried to get out — but I couldn't."

He looked away.

I tried to see his eyes. Were they blue?

Or yellow?

I couldn't see. It was too dark. Behind him, his reflections all looked away too.

I had to see his eyes. I had to know. Blue or yellow?

Is this really Fred? I wondered.

Or is this another monster trying to get out of the mirror?

Suddenly, I had an idea.

I clenched my fist. "Think fast!" I shouted.

I threw a punch at Fred's face.

He ducked — and staggered back, raising his hands to protect himself.

Yes! Good old wimpy Fred.

"It's you!" I cried happily.

"Of course it's me," he said, rolling his eyes. Blue eyes. "Now, are we going to get out of here or what?"

Holding Buzzy against my chest, I spun around slowly, searching for a path, an opening between the mirrors, any way to escape.

"We're completely surrounded by mirrors," Fred moaned.

"There's *got* to be a way out," I said. I slapped my hand angrily against a mirror.

To my surprise, the mirror slid back.

"I guess I should have tried that," Fred said, frowning.

I gave the mirror another push and made a space between the panes of glass big enough for us to slip through. Peering through the opening, I saw a path, rising up steeply, surrounded on both sides by mirrors.

"I fell a long way to get down here," I told Fred. "Maybe this path leads back up to my room."

Holding the dog in front of me, I squeezed through the narrow opening. Fred followed closely, and we began to climb.

The path grew steeper, and the air grew colder. Our shoes slipped and slid on the glassy surface of the floor. We leaned forward and trudged uphill slowly, carefully, a step at a time.

"I — I'm shivering," Fred whispered. "It's so cold."

The path grew even steeper. The glass all around us was covered with a thick layer of frost.

My teeth began to chatter. I held Buzzy close to keep us both warm.

Finally, the path straightened out. We found ourselves walking through a bright, shiny tunnel that sparkled as if lit by a million crystals. So bright I had to squint.

Up ahead, I could see a dark rectangle. Breathing hard, our breath fogging up in front of us, we reached the rectangle.

And stared out at my room!

"We made it!" I gasped, shivering, holding Buzzy against my chest.

I took a step toward my room — and my head hit solid glass.

"Ow!" I rubbed my forehead.

Fred pressed his hands against the wall of glass.

I stared out at my dresser, my wrestling posters. My room — so close and yet so far away.

I set Buzzy down and pressed my shoulder against the glass. Fred and I both ran our hands over it, searching desperately for an open space.

No. No way. The glass was solid.

"We have to g-get out of here! I'm f-freezing!" Fred cried, hugging himself.

"We don't have anything to break the glass," I said. "We need to break the mirror to —"

My words caught in my throat as I saw someone come through the door to my room. Claudia!

Claudia stepped through the doorway, and her eyes darted around the room, searching for me, I guessed.

"Over here!" I shouted. "Claudia — look over here!"

"Help us! Help us out of here!" Fred cried.

We both pounded our fists on the glass.

"Claudia — look into the mirror!" I screamed.

"Can't you hear us? Don't you see us? Look over here!"

I pounded the glass so hard, my fists ached. Claudia walked over to my desk. I saw her pick something up. She turned to leave.

"My Game Boy! I don't believe it! I told her she couldn't borrow it unless she asked me!"

"Come back!" Fred screamed to her. "Come back! We're freezing in here!"

Claudia turned. Her eyes swept the room one more time.

Did she hear us?

Did she see us?

No. She walked out, studying the Game Boy.

"No! Noooooo!" Fred howled.

I let out a long, miserable sigh.

"Now what? How are we going to get out of this mirror?" Fred asked, shivering.

"I — I don't know," I whispered.

I shoved my cold hands deep into my pants pockets — and suddenly, I knew what I had to do.

My fingers wrapped around the handle of the pocket mirror. I completely forgot that I had it.

I pulled out the mirror and showed it to Fred. "This can help us. I know it can."

Fred frowned at it. "How?"

Holding the handle tightly, I slammed the little mirror into the wall of glass.

It made a loud *CRASH*. But not a dent in the glass.

I smashed it into the glass again.

Again.

"Give up, Jason," Fred whispered. "There's no way you can break through."

I spun around. The little mirror pointed at Fred.

I saw his reflection in the glass. Then, suddenly, I was staring at *two* Freds!

I trained the mirror on Fred again — and made a third Fred appear.

"Hey — stop!" the real Fred cried.

But there were already five Freds standing next to him. They all blinked and gazed around, testing their arms and legs, surprised and bewildered.

"Come on — push!" I ordered them. "Everybody push against the glass."

I figured seven of us were stronger than only two.

We all leaned our shoulders against the mirror glass and pushed. We groaned and strained.

The big pane of glass didn't budge. Didn't bend or give way.

"A hundred Freds couldn't break this thing!" Fred cried. "It's as strong as steel!"

The other Freds shrugged their shoulders and walked away, disappearing into the mist.

"Now what?" Fred sighed. "We — we're going to freeze to death in here."

I glanced down at poor little Buzzy. The dog had curled himself into a tight ball, struggling to keep warm. He gazed up at me with pleading eyes, as if asking me to do something to help him.

I spun the mirror around and aimed it at the glass.

To my surprise, the glass made a sizzling sound. Steam rose off it.

I kept the little mirror trained on the glass. The sizzling grew louder.

101

A small round hole opened in the glass.

I aimed the mirror steadily ahead of me.

The hole grew bigger.

Bigger . . .

Big enough for us to slip through?

Yes!

Fred moved first. He lowered his shoulder and carefully edged through the opening. He pushed out of the mirror and landed heavily on my bedroom floor.

"Hurry, Jason!" he called.

He didn't have to tell me to hurry. I grabbed up Buzzy and pushed him through the opening. Then I slid out too, gasping at the shock of warmth as I stepped into my room.

Struggling to catch my breath, I turned back in time to see the mirror close up.

"I'm outta here, Jason!" Fred cried. "My parents must be so worried!"

He tore out of the room. I heard his shoes pounding down the stairs. The front door slammed after him.

Wagging his stubby tail, Buzzy took off too. I guess he wanted to get as far away from that mirror as he could.

So did I.

Were Mom and Dad home?

I started to the door.

But I stopped halfway across the room when someone stepped into the doorway.

I blinked in surprise. "Claudia? Is that you?"

No. Not Claudia.

My mouth dropped open in horror as I stared at *myself*.

Me — walking quickly into my room.

"No!" I gasped. "You're not me!"

The other figure stopped and gazed at me. His face showed no surprise. A cold grin spread slowly over his face.

"I *am* you now, Jason," he said softly. "You live in the mirror. And I live on the outside now. I'm Jason now. And I'm going to stay Jason from now on."

"No —" I protested. But my shout came out weak and trembling. "You can't do this! I'm not going back into that mirror."

His grin grew wider. "What do you plan to do? Fight me? You know I'm stronger than you, Jason. You know you can't beat me."

His arms slid into his body. The giant crablike claws began to pull out from his shoulders.

"Why not go peacefully, Jason? Go back in the

mirror. I won't let you stay out here. I took over your life as soon as you went into the mirror. And I'm going to keep it."

As he lumbered toward me, his mouth gaped wide, wider, until he swallowed his head once again. The monstrous red inside-out face glared at me now with its bulging yellow eyeballs.

Trembling, I took a step back.

"Back in the mirror," he growled, advancing on me. "Back in the mirror — now!"

I glanced around frantically for something I could throw, something I could swing at him. My eyes stopped on the hand mirror. I still gripped it in my hand!

Yes!

The mirror will defeat him, I told myself.

The mirror will send the monster back where he belongs.

My hand trembled, but I swung the mirror up. Swung it up and aimed it at the monster's face.

He uttered a low growl.

Then he swiped a big claw — and batted the mirror easily from my fingers.

And moved in for the kill.

33

"**N**ooooo!"

I screamed as he tightened a claw around my waist and lifted me into the air. I twisted and squirmed.

He pulled the claw back, preparing to throw me into the mirror.

I can't go back there, I told myself.

I can't let him *steal* my life!

The creature's sharp claw cut into my skin as it tightened around my waist.

He raised me higher. Higher.

"Noooo!" Another shrill scream escaped my throat.

I reached for his face. I raked frantically at his wet red cheeks.

It didn't hurt him. He didn't react at all.

I pounded his fat nose with my fist.

He lumbered toward the mirror.

I'm doomed, I realized. Doomed . . .

My fists frantically punched his face. I tugged the spongelike nose.

Then I gripped his bulging yellow tennis ball eyes.

I gripped them hard — *and pulled them out!*

"Unnnnnnnnnh!" A shuddering moan rose up from the creature.

The claw slid open, and I fell to the floor.

Groaning and whimpering, the monster doubled over in pain. Yellow slime spewed from his empty eye sockets. He buried his face behind his claws.

"Unnnh . . . unnnh . . . unnnnnh."

As the big creature collapsed, I jumped to my feet. I dove quickly behind him.

And shoved him with both hands.

Shoved him hard — into the mirror.

He staggered forward, through the glass, into the cold mirror world, still doubled over, still moaning in agony.

"No more!" I screamed. "No more!"

In a fury, I picked up the big brass lamp from my bed table. I yanked the wire from the wall.

Ran across the room.

Raised the lamp high.

I saw Mom at the bedroom door. I saw the shocked look on her face.

But I didn't care.

I heaved the lamp at the mirror.

The glass shattered loudly. Shattered into a million pieces.

The pieces fell to my bedroom floor.

I stood there, struggling to catch my breath, trying to slow my racing heart.

"Jason —" Mom started. "What on earth?"

"It's over," I whispered. "I'm okay now, Mom. It's over."

Mom stood staring at me, openmouthed.

Claudia stepped into the room behind her. "What's going on in here, Jason? What's all the noise?"

Claudia stopped when she saw the shards of glass over my floor. Her mouth dropped open too. "Uh-oh, Jason. A broken mirror. Don't you know that's seven years bad luck?"

I didn't try to explain to Mom and Dad. I knew they'd never believe me.

They helped me clean up my room. And when I told them not to worry, that it would never happen again, they were kind enough not to ask any questions.

I had my own questions. What happened to the Fred and Buzzy monsters? Did they go back to the mirror world when the real Fred and Buzzy escaped? I hoped so.

For now, I concentrated on cleaning up. The yellow slime was impossible to get off the carpet. No matter how hard we scrubbed, the stains just wouldn't come up.

When we were finally finished scrubbing and vacuuming, I hung two wrestling posters on the wall where the mirror used to be.

I sat down on my bed, feeling tired but relieved.

Something on the desk caught my eye. I grabbed it and took a quick look at it.

The stained warning note: BEWARE. BRING THIS INTO YOUR HOUSE — AND YOU BRING DEATH.

"I don't need this anymore," I said out loud. I crumpled it up and tossed it in the wastebasket.

I glanced out the window at the sunny day. I wondered how Fred was doing. I wondered if he felt as happy as I did.

I picked up the phone and started to punch in his number.

But I stopped when I saw something move across the room.

The bottom drawer of the old antique dresser. The drawer that had been stuck.

I stared in shock as the drawer slid out a few inches. It creaked as it slid.

A brown head poked up from the dresser drawer. A snake head, only much bigger, *as big as a human head.*

A slender brown creature slithered up from the drawer. It had the body of a snake and moved like a snake, but it was covered in thick, matted brown fur.

I dropped the phone. And stumbled back onto my bed.

"Hey!" The snake jaw snapped open. "Hey —" the creature whispered, its furry tongue slapping the roof of its mouth. "Hey — did you get my note?"

About the Author

R.L. Stine is the most popular author in America. He is the creator of the *Goosebumps*, *Give Yourself Goosebumps*, *Fear Street*, and *Ghosts of Fear Street* series, among other popular books. He has written over 250 scary novels for kids. Bob lives in New York City with his wife, Jane, teenage son, Matt, and dog, Nadine.